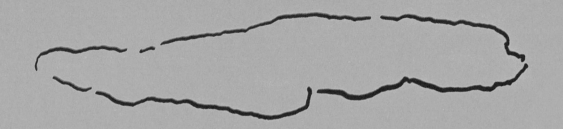

Bears in my bed

To my mother and father.
M.I.

10 9 8 7 6 5 4 3 2 1
First published in the United Kingdom in 2000
by David Bennett Books Limited, United Kingdom.
Distributed by Sterling Publishing Company, Inc. 387, Park Avenue South, New York,
N.Y. 10016. Distributed in Canada by Sterling Publishing, c/o Canadian Manda Group,
One Atlantic Avenue, Suite 105, Toronto, Ontario, Canada M6K 3E7.

Text and illustrations copyright © 2000 Michael Irwin.
Style and design copyright © 2000 David Bennett Books Limited.

Michael Irwin asserts his moral right to be
identified as the author and illustrator of this work.

ISBN 0-8069-7535-0
Printed in China.

Bears in my bed

by Michael Irwin

I've got bears
in my bed!

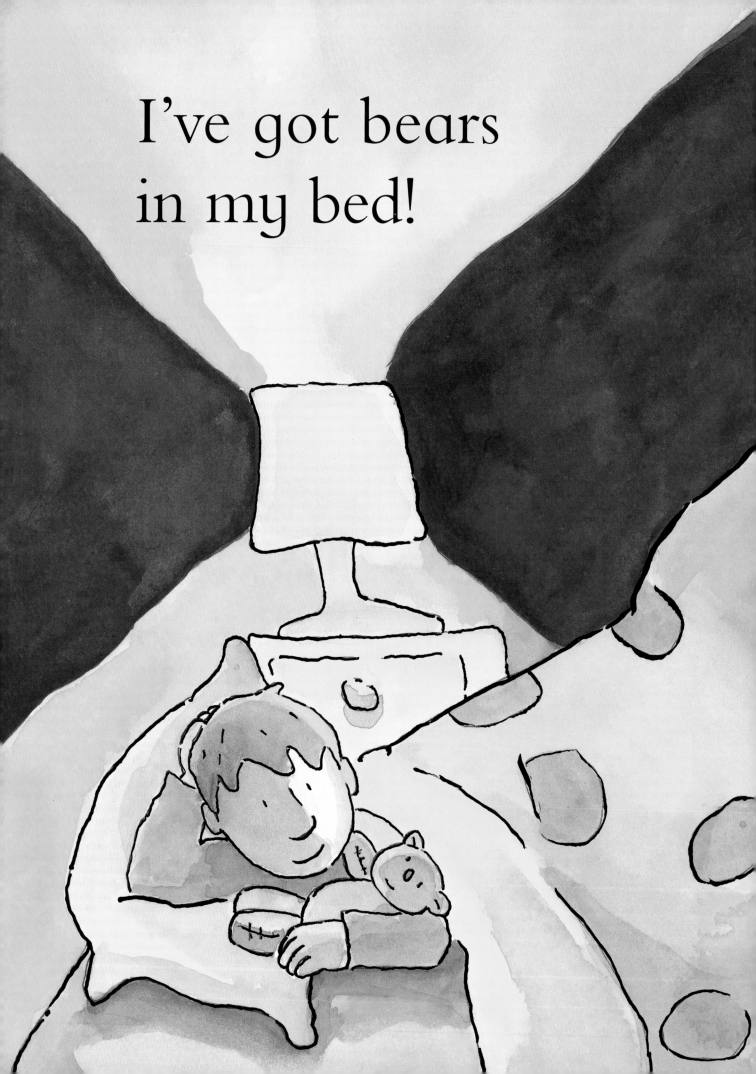

I woke up one morning
to find them there.
They don't talk,
just sit and stare...

My Mom says,
"Thomas, it's all
in your head!"

But at night, I have
bears in my bed.

Last night they even threatened Ted!

They're always
under my feet
and dribble
when I eat.

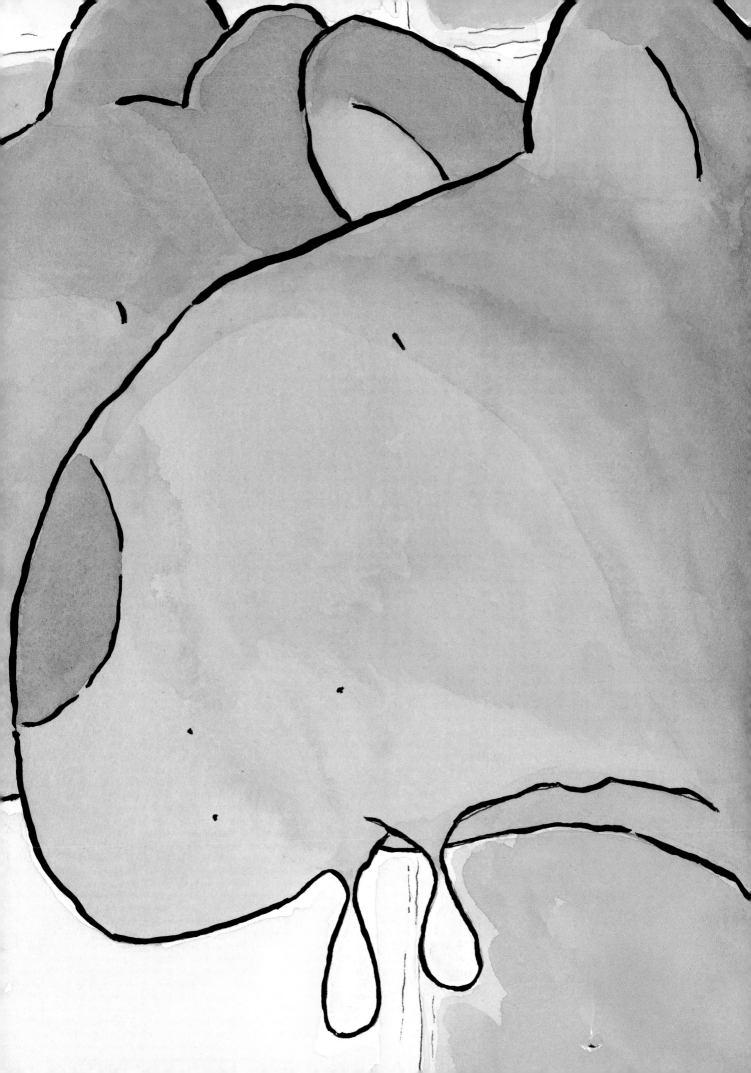

They have to go!
But how? They could
live in the garden...

...it's small and square. But they might not like it because our rabbits live there.

There's always our car.
That would get them
quite far...

...through leafy lanes, over hills and away. But Mom says we need it for shopping today.

I know what to do!
I'll need one pot of
honey – not the hard
but the runny.

They can follow
my trail to
the zoo!

So now I no longer
have bears
in my bed…

...today I have
an elephant instead!